This book belongs to

_____

children's
choice®

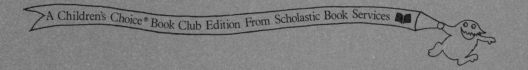

by BERNARD WABER

Lyle, Lyle, Crocodile

Houghton Mifflin Company, Boston

for Mary K.

Copyright © 1965 by Bernard Waber
Printed in the U.S.A.
ISBN: 0-590-75816-0

This is the house.
The house on
East 88th Street.
Mr. and Mrs. Primm
and their son Joshua
live in the house
on East 88th Street.
So does Lyle.
Listen:
SWISH, SWASH,
SPLASH, SWOOSH!
That's Lyle . . .

50071

3

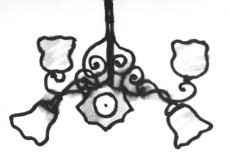

Lyle the crocodile.

Lyle was very happy living with the Primm family.

He was especially happy when he was being useful . . .
like helping Joshua brush up on school work.

But if Lyle was happy, he was making someone
else unhappy; perfectly miserable in fact.
That someone else was Loretta, Mr. Grumps' cat.
Mr. Grumps lived just two houses away from the Primms.
Whenever his cat caught even the slightest glimpse
of Lyle, she would fling herself into a nervous fit.

Lyle wanted desperately to win Loretta over.
He tried flashing his sweetest, most toothsome
smile at her to show how really friendly he was.
But this only frightened the distrustful
animal even more.

In the end, Mr. Grumps, who was even
more excitable than his cat, would burst from
the house shaking an angry fist at Lyle.
"Something will have to be done about that
crocodile," he shouted as Lyle fled
to the safety of his own house.

To take his mind off his troubles
with Loretta and Mr. Grumps, Lyle filled
his days playing with Joshua and his friends.
He loved being "it."

He could skip double-dutch
one hundred times without missing.

It came as no particular surprise
that Lyle could high-jump.
But Loretta, who was just let
out for an airing, was surprised.
She was terribly surprised.

Loretta was so surprised
and so shaken, she fled to
the nearest tree and
no amount of coaxing would
bring her down. Not until
Mr. Grumps arrived to
rescue and comfort her,
would she consider
coming down.

"Something will have to be done about
that crocodile," stormed Mr. Grumps.
Now Mr. Grumps was really furious.
Now he knew he would be snappy, irritable
and impossible to live with when he
returned to his job in a big department
store the following day.

For the next several days Mrs. Primm thought it best
to keep Lyle close at her side.
Together they fussed about the kitchen, preparing
good things for the family to eat.

When the weather permitted,
they took lunch to the park.

Lyle was always one for sharing.

They even took trips downtown.
There was much to see in the big city . . .
and much to do.

Mrs. Primm could spend hours
just browsing around antique shops.

Lyle could spend hours
watching building construction.

They both loved to ice-skate.

One day Mrs. Primm and Lyle went shopping
in a big department store. Unfortunately for
everyone, it turned out to be the very same store
in which Mr. Grumps held an important position.

And unfortunately, they were to hear from Mr. Grumps all too soon. For it was his voice that suddenly broke in over the loudspeaker to announce a sale in the pajama department.

Immediately, it was as if everyone in the store
was in desperate need of pajamas.
Separated from Mrs. Primm, Lyle was
swept along with the crowd.

As they neared the pajama department,
Lyle thought he heard a familiar voice.
"Lyle, Lyle," the voice called out.
Lyle recognized the voice all right . . .

. . . and the face as well.
The voice and the face belonged to
Hector P. Valenti, star of stage and screen.
But what was Signor Valenti up to now?
Well, for the moment it seemed,
he was very busy selling pajamas.

Lyle remembered unhappily his days of traveling
and performing with Signor Valenti.
But in spite of everything, the two were
delighted to see each other once more.

50071

In another part of the store, Mrs. Primm
searched frantically for Lyle.
"Excuse me," she said to the lady at
the information booth, "have you seen a
crocodile going past? He was wearing a red scarf."
"No," answered the lady. "I have no information
about a crocodile wearing a red scarf."

"Excuse me," said Mrs. Primm to the sporting goods salesman, "have you by chance come across a crocodile? His name is Lyle."
"Sorry, madam," answered the salesman, "I have not come across any crocodiles named Lyle today."

s. Primm grew more and more upset.
xcuse me," she said to a man wearing a
ite carnation, "I have lost my crocodile
d I don't know what to do."
natever the man answered, Mrs. Primm never
ard it, for his voice was lost in a chorus
other voices shouting, "More, more!"

Those voices belonged to the huge crowd of shoppers
surrounding Hector P. Valenti and Lyle.
Because they had an audience, and because Signor
Valenti could not resist showing off, he had
persuaded Lyle to join him in a free performance
of their old stage act.
"More, more!" the surprised, but delighted
shoppers called out, forgetting all about
wanting or even needing pajamas.

Mrs. Primm caught up with them just in time
to hear still another voice, charged with fury,
shout, "What is going on here?"
This was Mr. Grumps.
And when Mr. Grumps saw what was really going on
his face turned red, blue and purple with rage.
"Madam," he gasped, "we do not permit crocodiles
in this store you know. Remove him at once!!
And you sir," he said, pointing a daggerlike finger
at Signor Valenti, "you sir, are dismissed!!"

"Something will have to be done about that crocodile."
Those warning words of Mr. Grumps still rang in
their ears as they said goodbye to Signor Valenti
outside the store.

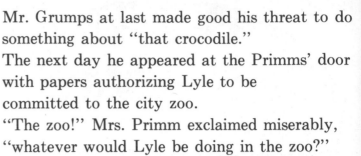

Mr. Grumps at last made good his threat to do something about "that crocodile."
The next day he appeared at the Primms' door with papers authorizing Lyle to be committed to the city zoo.
"The zoo!" Mrs. Primm exclaimed miserably, "whatever would Lyle be doing in the zoo?"
"He'll be doing whatever it is normal crocodiles are supposed to be doing," snapped Mr. Grumps who wasn't being at all nice about it.
The Primms examined the papers.
They appeared to be in order.

There was little they could do, at least for the moment,
to prevent Mr. Grumps from putting Lyle in the zoo.

Lyle's first night
was difficult indeed.

Not wanting to seem unsociable, he decided
to join the other crocodiles
who were cozily piled together.
Just when he thought he had gotten
himself comfortable on top . . .

he awakened to find himself crushed to the very bottom.

Lyle's restlessness so annoyed the other crocodiles,
they all just got up and stomped off in a huff.

Lyle was happier during the day, when visitors
came. He amused everyone with his unusual tricks
and before long was the biggest attraction at the zoo.

Joshua and Mrs. Primm visited regularly,
arms laden with games, toys and the Turkish
caviar Lyle so loved.
Mrs. Primm did her best to smile
and appear cheerful, but just couldn't hide
her concern.
"Are you feeling all right dear?" she would ask.
"Are you getting enough rest?
Are you making friends with the
other crocodiles?
Do the lions keep you awake at night?
Is the floor too damp?
Do the flies pester you?"
Lyle shook his head yes or no, depending on
the question. He tried putting on a brave
front, but Mrs. Primm knew very well he was
unhappy and fought back her tears.

One night a new keeper appeared at Lyle's cage.
Surprise! Surprise!
The new keeper turned out to be
none other than
Hector P. Valenti, star of stage and screen.
"Sh!" whispered Signor Valenti,
"I have come to rescue you."
Signor Valenti unlocked the door of the cage
and an astonished Lyle was set free.

"You can't go home again," said Signor Valenti
when they had put the zoo behind them.
Signor Valenti was bursting with ideas.
"We'll put our old act together again," he said.
"We'll fly to Australia. They'll love us in Australia."
Lyle groaned. The very thought of never seeing the
house on East 88th Street again was grim indeed
and too much for him to endure.

Signor Valenti read his thoughts and decided
Lyle should have one last look at the house on
East 88th Street.
Approaching the now sleeping street, they were
suddenly met with a wall of dense smoke.
The smoke, they realized with horror, was coming
from Mr. Grumps' house.
While Signor Valenti ran to signal the alarm,
Lyle broke into the house and rescued the
still sleeping occupants.

A gasping, frightened Mr. Grumps and his cat
were led to the safety of the street.

Now the Primms and the entire neighborhood were awake
and witness to Lyle's heroism. Mr. Grumps
couldn't thank him enough.
"Ladies and gentlemen," said Mr. Grumps to the crowd
of onlookers, "Lyle is the bravest, kindest, most
wonderful crocodile in the whole, wide world. I would
consider it a privilege and a pleasure to have him
as our neighbor once more."
"Hooray!" shouted the Primms.
"Hooray!" shouted the crowd.

Lyle moved back to the house
on East 88th Street that very night.

Several days later, a farewell party was given
by the Primms for Signor Valenti, who was leaving
to seek fortune and adventure in Australia.
"Remember," said Mr. Grumps, speaking to Signor Valenti,
"should you change your mind about leaving, a job in
my store will always be yours just for the asking.
We need people with your kind of talent and ability."
Everyone smiled happily . . .

. . . even Loretta.

Look Who's Part of the Children's Choice® Family!

Something special for Children's Choice® Book Club members

You can get all these storybook favorites—Puss in Boots, Babar, Curious George, Lyle, George and Martha and The Year at Maple Hill Farm—to hang up on your wall. They're big (17″ × 22″) and beautiful posters, printed in full color on high quality paper. Best of all, you can get all 6 for just $3.95, including postage and handling.

To order your set of 6 Children's Choice® posters, please send your name, address and $3.95 in check or money order to:

CHILDREN'S CHOICE®POSTERS
2931 East McCarty St.
P.O. Box 1068
Jefferson City, Mo. 65102

Please allow 3-6 weeks for delivery. Your posters are mailed in a tube, so they won't be creased at all.

Offer expires August 31, 1981

ADVERTISEMENT